MW00761662

Grandma Loves You!

To Jean Ferris and her grandson, EJ.

—Helen Foster James

To Pat and Bill, thanks for everything x

— Petra Brown

Sleeping Bear Press
2395 South Huron Parkway, Suite 200
Ann Arbor, MI 48104
www.sleepingbearpress.com

Printed and bound in the United States.

20 19 18 17 16

Library of Congress Cataloging-in-Publication Data

James, Helen Foster, 1951-
Grandma loves you! / written by Helen Foster James; illustrated by Petra Brown.
pages cm
Summary: A rabbit grandmother welcomes an infant that she has loved from the start, and not just because the little one is her own baby's baby.
ISBN 978-1-58536-836-5
[1. Stories in rhyme. 2. Grandmothers–Fiction. 3. Babies–Fiction. 4. Rabbits–Fiction.] I. Brown, Petra, illustrator. II. Title.
PZ8.3.J1477Gr 2013
[E]–dc23
2013002582

This book is presented to:

On this day:

Grandma

Written by Helen Foster James

Loves You!

Illustrated by Petra Brown

The moment I saw you,
I fell in love,

Honey, my bunny,
my sweet turtledove.

Wiggling and giggling,
you captured my heart.

I loved you so much, dear,
right from the start.

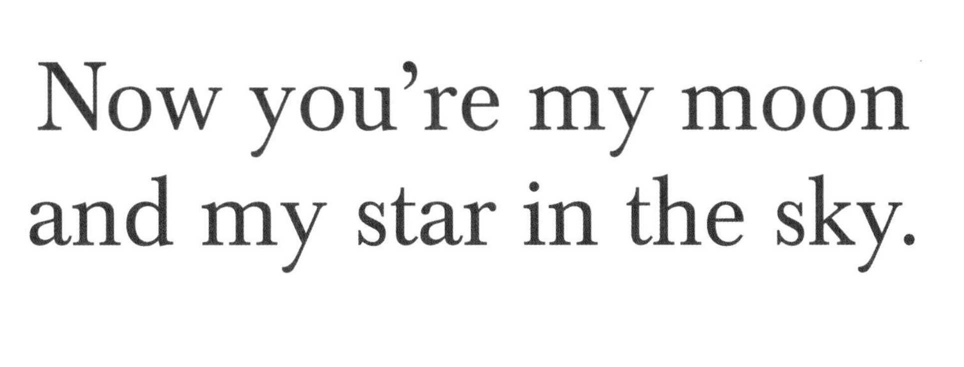

Now you're my moon
and my star in the sky.

My sweet, little pea,
my sugar plum pie.

I hold you and hug you,
my cupcake, my dear.

I whisper, “I love you”
in your little ear.

I tickle your toes
and you hold my hand.

You are the reason
that I am called "grand."

Grandmama loves you,
my cute little one.

Honey, my bunny,
my bundle of fun.

My baby grew up,
and now there is you.

For you are my baby's baby,
that's true.

So here is my promise
I want you to know:

I'll love you forever,
wherever you go.

A Special Letter to My Grandchild

With Love,

Paste a picture of grandma
and grandchild here.